Little Goose
Goes Out of Step

Jean-François Dumont

A new day on the farm and the animals are waking up.

At the top of the hill, the geese gather for their long march down to the pond for their morning wash.

One,   One,   One,
    Two,   Two,   Two

Igor, who's in charge, sets the pace.

One,   One,   **One**,
    Two,   Two,   **Two**

The sound gets louder…

Webbed feet hit the ground together.
Bottoms waggle from side to side.
Step matches step.

Igor is happy.

The geese always march like this.
No one quite knows why.

Edgar the rat thinks
it must help them to brave the cold pond.
Igor just says: "It's a tradition."
It makes him feel proud.

One,   One,   One,   One,
     Two;   Two;   Two splat;   Two splat;

Igor listens hard.

                                 One,   One,
                                   Two splat;   Two splat;

Igor frowns.

"What's that noise? That 'splat' noise?"

He's not happy.

One,
Two splat;
One,
Two splat;
One,
Two splat;
One,
Two splat;

This won't do at all.
Igor orders the geese to STOP!

Igor stomps along the line
until he finds a little goose
who's blushing and looking down at her feet.

"Zita!" roars Igor.
"Is it you making that noise?"

Zita wants to say that she can't help it,

that she's new to the group,

that a noisy cow put her off,

but Igor's not interested.

He sends Zita back to the farm.

As she slinks away,

she hears the other geese march off.

One.   One.   One.
    Two,   Two,   Two

A little later, Zita sets off for the pond again.

"I'm rubbish at being a goose," she thinks.

"It can't be that hard to march in step."

One,   One,   One,
      Two,   Two,   Two

One,   One,   One,
      Two,   Two,   Two

"Even silly Annabel can do it."

She feels like crying.

One,   One,   One,
     Two,   Two,   Two

"Why can't I be like the others?"

One,   One,   One,
     Two,   Two,   Two

"They always get it right!"

On the way to the pond,

Zita passes a pair of piglets, Rosie and Bruno.

"Hey, isn't that the new goose?" asks Bruno.

"Why isn't she with the others?"

"Yes, that's her," says Rosie.

"Looks like she's crying."

Zita ignores them.

She's still worrying about marching.

"It's not hard," she thinks, "so why can't I do it?"

Splat, splosh and splash **sniff** splosh

go her webbed feet on the ground.

"I can't even walk right," she mutters.

Splat **sniff** splosh and splash **sniff** splosh

Splat **sniff** splosh and splash **sniff** splosh **sniff** splash

"Wow! That's a cool tune," thinks a woodpecker
as Zita walks past.
He joins in, making sounds with his beak.

Splat **sniff** splosh tock and **sniff** splash tock **sniff,** splosh tock
Splat **sniff** splosh tock and **sniff** splash tock **sniff,** splosh tock

Zita walks past Ray the chicken.

"Yeah!" he thinks, "That music makes me feel
like shaking my tail!"

He joins in as well.

cluck cluck cluck cluck cluck cluck   cluck cluck cluck cluck cluck cluck cluck
splash **sniff**   splash tock   and **sniff**   splash, tock **sniff** splash tock

cluck cluck cluck cluck cluck cluck   cluck cluck cluck cluck cluck cluck cluck
splash **sniff**   splash tock   and **sniff**   splash, tock **sniff** splash tock

"That little goose sure can swing!"
think the donkey and the cow.
And they add some sounds too.

cluck cluck cluck cluck cluck cluck cluck cluck cluck cluck cluck cluck cluck

splash sniff   splash tock and sniff   splash, tock sniff splash tock

heeeeeeehaaaawwwww   Moooooooooooooooooooooooo

"Mmm! Groovy!" thinks Denise the ewe.
"If I had fingers I'd be clicking them!"

cluck cluck cluck. cluck cluck cluck   cluck cluck cluck cluck cluck cluck cluck

splash **sniff**   splash tock and **sniff**   splash, tock **sniff** splash tock

heeeeeehaaaawwwwww   **Moooooooooooooooooooo**

Baaaaa Baaaaa Baaaaa Baaaaa Baaaaa Baaaaa

When Zita arrives at the pond,
Igor can't believe his eyes.
The most amazing parade.
And everyone dancing in rhythm.
Everyone together!

Now no one marches except Igor.

He still does the old One, One,
Two, Two.

Everyone else waits for Zita.
She dances to a different tune every day!

First published in Great Britain in 2009 by Zero To Ten Limited
2A Portman Mansions, Chiltern Street,
London W1U 6NR

This edition © 2009 Zero To Ten Limited
© Père Castor Flammarion, 2007

First published in France in 2007 as La petite oie qui ne voulait
pas marcher au pas
by Jean-François Dumont

Translated by Nicola Edwards

British Library Cataloguing in Publication Data:

Dumont, Jean-Francois, 1959-

  Little Goose goes out of step

  1. Geese - Pictorial works - Juvenile fiction 2. Children's
  stories - Pictorial works
  I. Title
  843.9'2[J]

ISBN-13: 9781840895407

Printed in Dubai